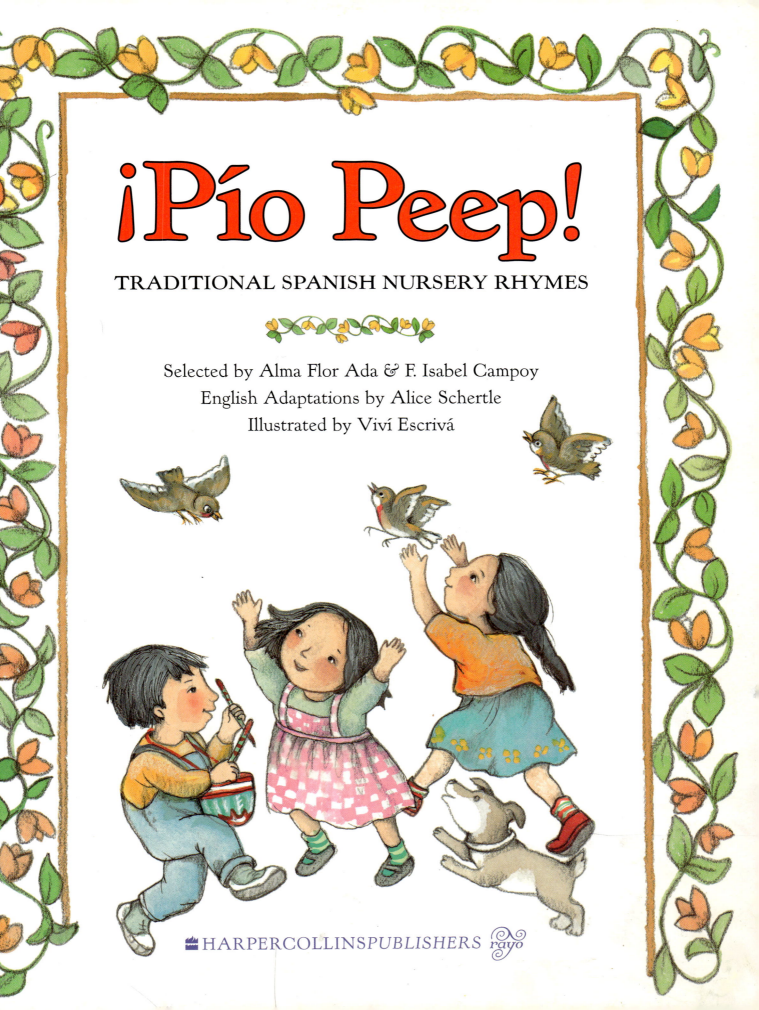

¡Pío Peep!

TRADITIONAL SPANISH NURSERY RHYMES

Selected by Alma Flor Ada & F. Isabel Campoy
English Adaptations by Alice Schertle
Illustrated by Viví Escrivá

HARPERCOLLINSPUBLISHERS rayo

Library of Congress Cataloging-in-Publication Data
Pío peep! : traditional Spanish nursery rhymes / selected by Alma Flor Ada & F. Isabel Campoy ;
English adaptations by Alice Schertle ; illustrated by Viví Escrivá.
    p.   cm.
Summary: A collection of more than two dozen nursery rhymes in Spanish, from
Spain and Latin America, with English translations.
ISBN 0-688-16019-0 – ISBN 0-688-16020-4 (lib. bdg.)
1. Nursery rhymes, Spanish.   2. Nursery rhymes, Spanish American.   [1. Nursery rhymes.
2. Spanish language materials–Bilingual.]   I. Ada, Alma Flor.   II. Campoy, F. Isabel.
III. Schertle, Alice.   IV. Escrivá, Viví, ill.
PZ74.3 .P52   2003   398.8–dc21   2001051641

Typography by Matt Adamec
4 5 6 7 8 9 10
❖
First Edition

Para Camila Rosa, Cristina Isabel,
Daniel Antonio, Jessica Emilia, Nicolás, Samantha Rosa,
Timoteo Pablo y Victoria Ana Zubizarreta
y para Rebecca Sofía Chang-Martínez.
—A.F.A. and F.I.C.

To Jen, Drew, Kate, and John
—A.S.

Spanish oral folklore is rich in nursery rhymes and songs. Some rhymes are fragments of ancient medieval ballads; others, such as *De colores*, are old harvest songs. Some are frequently sung as lullabies, like *Este niño lindo*, others as finger plays, like *Palmas palmitas*.

Some rhymes accompany games, such as *El patio de mi casa*, while others are unending rhymes that can be repeated as long as the child wants, like *El barquito* or *La hormiguita*.

In most cases the rhymes and songs originated in Spain and crossed the Atlantic with the language, to delight children in all the nineteen Spanish-speaking countries of Latin America as well as the American Southwest, occasionally changing along the way. Of the ones we have collected here, three are from Mexico—*La víbora de la mar*, *La piñata*, and *Tortillitas*—the rest are well-known throughout the Spanish-speaking world. We have purposely selected some of the best known and most loved rhymes as an introduction to this genre.

To make the selection for this book, we reviewed numerous anthologies from Spain and Latin America, among them those of Carmen Bravo Villasante, Arturo Medina, and Ana Pellegrin in Spain; Elsa Isabel Bornemann and María Elena Walsh in Argentina; the series *Así cantan y juegan . . .*, published by CONAFE in Mexico, and many more. Finally, faced with the decision to select among hundreds, we chose those nursery rhymes and songs that we cherished in our own childhoods, and those the numerous children—Mexican, Puerto Rican, Cuban, Dominican, and Central American—with whom we have worked love the most.

Índice · Contents

Introducción

La palabra se hace canto y juego para los niños. Los acompaña mientras se duermen en brazos de la madre, galopan en las rodillas del padre, o descubren, con la abuelita, como jugar con los dedos.

El folklore hispánico es abundantísimo. En sus palabras aladas la cultura familiar se continúa de generación en generación. Algunas rimas y canciones se han mantenido casi idénticas en su largo peregrinar a ambos lados del Atlántico. Otras, se han enriquecido con la contribución de los distintos grupos que forman la cultura hispánica. Todas proporcionan deleite y encanto al acerbo común.

En el siglo XXI, esta riqueza cultural alcanza nuevas fronteras. Más de treinta y cinco millones de latinos aportan sus tradiciones al mosaico cultural de los Estados Unidos.

Esta pequeña muestra de esa riqueza se ofrece en dos idiomas para que sirva de vínculo de los niños latinos con su herencia y de enlace entre todos los niños de este país. El encanto de las rimas se ha mantenido en inglés al ofrecer no una traducción sino una recreación poética. En algunos casos se aparta de los detalles, pero respeta siempre la esencia original.

El folklore es frecuentemente el primer encuentro de los niños con la literatura. Puede ser, además, un excelente estímulo para la lectura. Ya sea que este libro facilite el que padres e hijos compartan una misma herencia o que aprendan a apreciar la cultura hispánica esperamos que los deleite.

Introduction

For children, words create a world of song and play. Words accompany children as they fall asleep in their mothers' arms, gallop upon their fathers' knees, or learn finger plays from their grandmothers.

Hispanic oral folklore is very rich. Its winged words have conveyed families' cultures and traditions from generation to generation. Some rhymes and songs have remained nearly intact along their extensive journeys on both sides of the Atlantic. Others have been enriched by the contributions of the various groups that make up the Hispanic world. All provide joy and delight in our heritage.

In the twenty-first century, this cultural wealth is reaching new frontiers. More than thirty-five million Latinos contribute their traditions to the cultural mosaic that is the United States.

This book offers a small sample of this wealth, presented in two languages so that it can be meaningful to both Spanish and English speakers. To preserve the charm of the original rhymes, the English version is not a translation but a poetic re-creation. In some instances, the details are different, but the re-creation remains true to the essence of the original.

Frequently, oral folklore serves as children's first encounter with literature. It can also stimulate children to learn to read. Whether this book helps children and parents share a common heritage, or helps them develop a greater appreciation for Hispanic culture, we hope it will bring delight to all.

Pito, pito, colorito

—Pito, pito, colorito,

¿dónde vas tú, tan bonito?

—Voy al campo de la era.

A la escuela verdadera.

Good Morning, Early Bird

Good morning, early bird, tiny delight.

Where are you going so busy and bright?

To school in the meadow: I'll add up the seeds

and study the spiders and measure the weeds.

A la rueda rueda

A la rueda rueda
de pan y canela.
Dame un besito
y vete a la escuela.
Y si no quieres ir:
¡Acuéstate a dormir!

Bread and Cinnamon

Bread and cinnamon,

this is the rule.

Give me a kiss

and hurry to school.

If you want to sleep instead,

I won't wake you, sleepyhead!

Cinco pollitos

Cinco pollitos
tiene mi tía:
Uno le canta,
otro le pía
y tres le tocan la chirimía.

Five Little Chicks

Rum-a-tum-tum, whistles and sticks,
my auntie makes music with five little chicks:
One is a singer,
another can hum,
three play the melody, rum-a-tum-tum.

Caracol, caracol

Caracol, caracol,

saca tus cuernos al sol.

To a Snail

Poke your head out, little one.

Time to say, "Good morning, Sun!"

Cinco lobitos

Cinco lobitos
tiene la loba.
Blancos y negros
detrás de la cola.

Cinco tenía
y cinco crió.
Y al pequenín
sopitas le dio.

Five Little Wolf Pups

Five little wolf pups
white and black,
each little pup
had a tail in back.

Mother made soup
for each little pup,
but the littlest wolf
just gobbled it up.

Almendras y turrón

Palmas, palmitas,
hongos y castañitas,
almendras y turrón
¡para mi niño son!

Almonds and Chestnuts

Pat-a-cake, pat-a-cake, cookies for sale,
almonds and chestnuts and figs in a pail.
Cinnamon, marshmallow, strawberry treat—
Mommy makes cookies for somebody sweet.

Tortillitas para mamá

Tortillitas para mamá
tortillitas para papá.
Las calentitas para mamá,
las doraditas para papá.

Tortillas for Mommy

Mommy likes tortillas
steaming hot and yummy.
Make them round and nicely browned
for Daddy's hungry tummy.

Aquí puso la pajarita el huevo

Aquí puso la pajarita el huevo.

Éste lo agarró,

éste lo partió,

éste lo cocinó,

éste le echó la sal,

y este pícaro gordo

se lo comió.

18

Here the Bird Laid the Egg

Here the bird laid one round egg.

This one found it,

this one cracked it,

this one cooked it,

this one put salt on it,

and this fat rascal

gobbled it up!

Aserrín, aserrán

Aserrín, aserrán,

los maderos de San Juan

piden pan, no les dan.

Piden queso, les dan hueso.

Aserrín, aserrán,

piden tortas, sí les dan

se las comen

y se van.

See-saw, See-Saw

See-saw, see-saw, come and gone,
all the woodsmen of San Juan.
If they ask for cheese and bread,
give them just a bone instead.

If they ask for chocolate cake,
how many pieces will they take?
See-saw, see-saw, come and gone,
all the woodsmen of San Juan.

De colores

De colores,
de colores
se visten los campos
en la primavera.

De colores,
de colores
son los pajaritos
que vienen de fuera.

De colores,
de colores
es el arco iris
que vemos lucir.

Y por eso los grandes amores
de muchos colores
me gustan a mí.

Many Colors

Many colors,
many colors,
the fields and the meadows
are dressing for spring.

Many colors,
many colors,
they flash from the feathers
of birds on the wing.

Many colors,
many colors,
see how they shine
in the rainbow above.

In the beautiful world all around me
these colors surround me,
these colors I love.

El patio de mi casa

El patio de mi casa
es particular.
Cuando llueve se moja
como los demás.

—Agáchate
y vuélvete a agachar
que los agachaditos
no saben bailar.

—Salta la tablita.
—Yo ya la salté.
Sáltala tú ahora.
Yo ya me cansé.

In My Backyard

In my backyard,
it's strange to say,
the grass gets wet
when it rains all day.

Drop down, drop down,
touch the floor.
Those who fall will
dance no more.

Jump it, jump it,
your turn soon—
over the table,
over the moon.

La hormiguita

Ésta era una hormiguita
que de su hormiguero
salió calladita
y entró en un granero.
Agarró un triguito
y salió ligero.

Salió otra hormiguita
del mismo hormiguero
y muy calladita
entró en el granero.
Agarró un triguito
y salió ligero.

Y salió otra hormiguita
del mismo hormiguero . . .

The Little Ant

The first little ant
came out of a hill
and crept to the barn, as still, as still . . .
She snatched one grain
of golden wheat
and tiptoed out on her little ant feet.

The second little ant
came out of a hill
and crept to the barn, as still, as still . . .
She snatched one grain
of golden wheat
and tiptoed out on her little ant feet.

The third little ant . . .

Caballito blanco

Caballito blanco
sácame de aquí,
llévame hasta el pueblo
donde yo nací.

—Tengo, tengo, tengo.
—Tú no tienes nada.
—Tengo tres ovejas
en una manada.

Una me da leche,
otra me da lana,
otra mantequilla
toda la semana.

Little White Pony

Little white pony,
wherever I roam,
gallop me, gallop me,
gallop me home.

I have a secret,
no secret at all—
three little lambs
who come when I call.

One gives me wool
that's softer than silk,
one gives me butter,
and one gives me milk.

Arroz con leche

Arroz con leche
me quiero casar
con una señorita
de la capital.
Que sepa coser,
que sepa bailar,
que sepa abrir la puerta
para ir a jugar.
Con ésta sí,
con ésta no,
con esta señorita
me caso yo.

Rice Pudding

Rice pudding, rice pudding,

it's married I'll be;

I'll find in the city

the right girl for me.

She'll sew and she'll dance

tap-a-tap on the floor;

she'll come out to play

when I knock on the door.

Say yes, say no,

say maybe instead.

If this one will have me,

I soon will be wed.

Los elefantes

Un elefante se balanceaba
sobre la tela de una araña.
Como veía que resistía
fue a llamar a otro elefante.

Dos elefantes se balanceaban
sobre la tela de una araña.
Como veían que resistía
fueron a llamar a otro elefante.

The Elephants

One brave elephant

swung on a silver thread.

"A web in a breeze is a lovely trapeze,

more elephants, please," he said.

Two brave elephants

swung on a silver thread.

"A web in a breeze is a lovely trapeze,

more elephants, please," they said.

Tres elefantes se balanceaban

sobre la tela de una araña.

Como veían que resistía

fueron a llamar a otro elefante.

Cuatro . . .

Three brave elephants
swung on a silver thread.
"A web in a breeze is a lovely trapeze,
more elephants, please," they said.

Four . . .

El barquito

Había una vez un barco chiquitico,

había una vez un barco chiquitico,

había una vez un barco chiquitico,

que no sabía, que no sabía, que no sabía navegar.

Pasaron una, dos, tres, cuatro, cinco, seis, siete semanas,

pasaron una, dos, tres, cuatro, cinco, seis, siete semanas,

pasaron una, dos, tres, cuatro, cinco, seis, siete semanas,

y el barquito, y el barquito, y el barquito, no podía navegar.

Y si la historia no te parece larga,

y si la historia no te parece larga,

y si la historia no te parece larga,

volveremos, volveremos, volveremos a empezar.

The Little Boat

There was, was, was
a little boat, boat, boat
who never, never, never
learned to float, float, float.

Weeks and weeks and weeks and weeks
and weeks and weeks went by.
He couldn't float—he wouldn't even
try, try, try.

And if this silly story doesn't
sink, sink, sink,
we'll have to tell it one more time,
I think, think, think.

Tengo una muñeca

Tengo una muñeca
vestida de azul
con zapatos blancos
y velo de tul.

Las medias caladas
estilo andaluz
y el traje escotado
con su canesú.

La saqué a paseo,
se me resfrió,
la metí en la cama
con mucho dolor.

My Little Doll

My little doll,
all dressed in blue,
has two white shoes
and a lace veil, too.

Fancy stockings,
beautiful clothes,
she's all dressed up
wherever she goes.

She caught a cold.
I put her to bed,
tucked in her blanket,
patted her head.

Esta mañanita
me ha dicho el doctor
que le dé jarabe
con un tenedor.

Dos y dos son cuatro,
cuatro y dos son seis,
seis y dos son ocho
y ocho dieciséis.

Y ocho veinticuatro
y ocho treinta y dos,
quiero a mi muñeca
con el corazón.

The doctor says syrup
makes colds go away.
I give her a forkful
or two each day.

I teach her how
to count by twos,
two hands, two feet,
and two white shoes.

One and one
and one are three.
I love my dolly
and she loves me.

A la víbora de la mar

A la víbora, víbora de la mar,

por aquí pueden pasar.

La de adelante corre mucho.

La de atrás se quedará.

Tras, tras, tras.

Una mexicana que fruta vendía,

ciruela, chabacano, melón y sandía.

Verbena, verbena, jardín de matatena,

Verbena, verbena, jardín de matatena.

Sea Serpent

Sea serpent, sea serpent, pass on through;
gates swing open just for you.
Those in front must run through fast;
gates will close upon the last.
Last, last, last.

A Mexican woman has fruit to sell,
melons, apricots, plums as well.
Flowers, bones, and river stones.
Flowers, bones, and river stones.

*Played like London Bridge, with children holding on
to the one under the bridge when the verse ends.*

La piñata

Ándale amigo, no te dilates
con la canasta de los cacahuetes.

Ándale amigo, sal del rincón
con la canasta de la colación.

No quiero oro, ni quiero plata,
lo que yo quiero es romper la piñata.

Dale, dale, dale,
no pierdas el tino,
mide la distancia
que hay en el camino.

The Piñata

Hurry, my friend, let the party begin;

bring the basket of peanuts and pour them in.

Hurry, my friend, don't try to hide;

bring the basket of candy and put it inside.

I don't want silver, I don't want gold.

I'll break you, piñata, and take what you hold.

Hit it and hit it,

swing it around,

ready, aim, *smack!*

—treats fall to the ground.

Teresa, la marquesa

Teresa, la marquesa,

tipití, tipitesa,

tenía una corona,

tipití, tipitona,

con cuatro campanillas,

tipití, tipitillas.

Teresa the Marquesa

Teresa the marquesa,

tippi, tippi, tesa,

walks with a jingle,

tippi, tippi, tingle,

bells on her crown,

tippi, tippi, town.

Cucú

Cucú, cantaba la rana,

cucú, debajo del agua,

cucú, pasó un caballero,

cucú, con capa y sombrero.

Cucú, pasó una señora,

cucú, con traje de cola,

cucú, pasó una criada,

cucú, llevando ensalada.

Cucú, pasó un marinero,

cucú, vendiendo romero,

cucú, le pidió un poquito,

cucú, para sus hijitos.

Cucú, no le quiso dar,

cucú, se puso a llorar.

Cucú, se metió en el agua,

cucú, se ha echado a nadar.

Ribbitt

ribbitt Froggy sings a song
ribbitt as he swims along.
ribbitt Here comes someone tall,
ribbitt hat and cape and all.
ribbitt What a funny dress!
ribbitt That's her tail, I guess.
ribbitt Someone bringing lunch,
ribbitt lettuce by the bunch.
ribbitt Sailor selling sweets.
ribbitt Froggies need to eat.
ribbitt See me on this log?
ribbitt I'm a hungry frog!
ribbitt Sailor walks on by.
ribbitt Froggy starts to cry.
ribbitt *SPLASH!* He swims along.
ribbitt Froggy sings a song.

49

El sol es de oro

El sol es de oro

la luna es de plata

y las estrellitas

son de hoja de lata.

The Sun's a Gold Medallion

The sun's a gold medallion.

The moon's a silver ball.

The little stars are only tin;

I love them best of all.

Angelitos descalzos

A las puertas del cielo
venden zapatos
para los angelitos
que están descalzos.

Barefoot Angels

By the golden gate of Heaven
they are selling boots and shoes.
Little barefoot angels
get to buy the ones they choose.

A dormir va la rosa

A dormir va la rosa
de los rosales;
a dormir va mi niño
porque ya es tarde.

Mi niño se va a dormir
con los ojitos cerrados.
Como duermen los jilgueros
encima de los tejados.

Now Softly the Roses

Now softly the roses
are falling asleep.
Now softly you're rocking
as shadows grow deep.

In moonlight the finch
on the chimney is dozing.
Now softly my little one's
sweet eyes are closing.

Pajarito que cantas

Pajarito que cantas
en la laguna,
no despiertes al niño
que está en la cuna.

La cuna de mi niño
se mece sola,
como en el campo verde
las amapolas.

Little Bird Singing

Little bird singing
here by the lake,
sing softly, sing softly,
or baby will wake.

Breezes are rocking
my little one's bed;
each poppy is nodding
its own sleepy head.

Los pollitos dicen

Los pollitos dicen:
"Pío, pío, pío"
cuando tienen hambre,
cuando tienen frío.

La gallina busca
el maíz y el trigo,
les da la comida
y les presta abrigo.

Bajo sus dos alas
acurrucaditos,
hasta el otro día
duermen los pollitos.

56

Wide-awake Chicks

Wide-awake chicks say,
Peep! Peep! Peep!
We're hungry! We're cold!
We won't go to sleep!

Mother hen scratches
for barley and seeds
and gives them the warmth
a little chick needs.

Under her wings,
cozy and warm,
wide-awake chicks
sleep until dawn.

Duérmete, mi niña

Duérmete, mi niña,
duérmete, mi amor,
duérmete, pedazo
de mi corazón.

Esta niña linda,
que nació de día,
quiere que la lleven
a la dulcería.

Esta niña linda,
que nació de noche,
quiere que la lleven
a pasear en coche.

Sleep Now, My Baby

Sleep now, my baby,
sleep now, my love.
Here in my heart,
sleep, little dove.

This pretty baby,
born with the sun,
wants someone to buy her
a cinnamon bun.

This pretty baby,
born with the stars,
wants to go riding
in wagons and cars.

Esta niña linda,
no quiere dormir,
porque no le traen
la flor del jardín.

Esta niña linda,
se quiere dormir.
Cierra los ojitos
y los vuelve a abrir.

This pretty baby
wants one red rose.
Now soft as its petals
her sweet eyes will close.

Sleep now, my baby,
sleep now, my dear.
When you awaken,
I will be here.

El gato de trapo

Éste era un gato

que tenía los pies de trapo

y la colita al revés.

¿Quieres que te lo cuente otra vez?

Raggedy Cat

Raggedy, raggedy, raggedy cat.

Feet all lumpy, tail all flat.

Say it again, just like that—

Raggedy, raggedy, raggedy cat!

Un ratoncito

Un ratoncito
iba cansado
y este cuentecito
se ha terminado.

A Sleepy Mouse

A sleepy mouse
began to snore.
This tale is told—
there is no more.

About the Authors

Alma Flor Ada has devoted her life to promoting cross-cultural understanding and peace through children's literature, as well as enabling children to learn about their cultural heritage. "The words of nursery rhymes and songs gave both wings and roots to my soul," she declares, "and for that reason, I enjoy finding ways to continue sharing these treasures with children." Alma Flor Ada delights in studying, collecting, and anthologizing folklore as well as retelling folktales. Director of the Center for Multicultural Literature for Children and Young Adults at the University of San Francisco, Alma Flor Ada is the recipient of numerous academic and literary awards. Among them are the American Library Association's Pura Belpré Award, the Christopher Award, Aesop's Accolade, Parents' Choice Honors, Latina Writers Award, José Martí World Awards, and the Marta Salotti Gold Medal.

F. Isabel Campoy, poet, playwright, storyteller, and researcher of Hispanic culture, has devoted her life to the world of words. As a linguist, she has published numerous articles and textbooks for and about English language learners and Spanish language learners. She is the co-author of *Puertas al sol* and *Gateways to the Sun,* a collection of children's books about art, theater, poetry, biography, and culture in the Hispanic world. Her book *Authors in the Classroom,* co-authored with Alma Flor Ada, presents her current work of educating teachers, parents, and children to become authors of books that reflect their life experiences. Affirming the value of folklore, she states, "The word, when sung, conveys the pleasure of rhythm, just like a beating heart!"

About the Adapter

Alice Schertle has written more than thirty books for children, including *William and Grandpa,* which was the recipient of the Christopher Award. Several of her most recent books are collections of poetry. "I find writing poetry difficult, absorbing, frustrating, satisfying, maddening, intriguing. . . . I love it," she says. "If, at the end of a day of pondering, discarding, rewriting line after line, I can read my poem and say to myself, 'This one works,' it's been a good day."

A graduate of the University of Southern California and a former elementary school teacher, Alice Schertle has three grown children and lives in New Salem, Massachusetts.

About the Illustrator

Viví Escrivá is a celebrated illustrator from Spain whose work is also popular in the United States and Europe. *¡Pío Peep!* is one of the many books on which she has collaborated with Alma Flor Ada. In addition to illustration and fine art, Viví Escrivá has crafted imaginative large marionettes. She is from a family of illustrators and lives in Madrid, Spain.